SHORT AND

A book of very short scary stories

LOUISE COOPER

SHORT AND SCARY!

A book of very short scary stories

OXFORD
UNIVERSITY PRESS

OXFORD
UNIVERSITY PRESS

Great Clarendon Street, Oxford OX2 6DP

Oxford University Press is a department of the University of Oxford.
It furthers the University's objective of excellence in research, scholarship,
and education by publishing worldwide in

Oxford New York

Auckland Cape Town Dar es Salaam Hong Kong Karachi
Kuala Lumpur Madrid Melbourne Mexico City Nairobi
New Delhi Shanghi Taipei Tokyo Toronto

With offices in

Argentina Austria Brazil Chile Czech Republic France Greece
Guatemala Hungary Italy Japan Poland Portugal Singapore
South Korea Switzerland Thailand Turkey Ukraine Vietnam

Oxford is a registered trade mark of Oxford University Press
in the UK and in certain other countries

British Library Cataloguing in Publication Data available

ISBN 978-0-19-278190-1

15 17 19 20 18 16 14

Printed in Great Britain

Illustrated by Chris Mould

Paper used in the production of this book is a natural,
recyclable product made from wood grown in sustainable forests.
The manufacturing process conforms to the environmental
regulations of the country of origin.

Contents

Sticky Ending (1)

L ittle boy.
Climbs a tree.
Branch goes SNAP.
R.I.P.

The Rain Tree

Mum, Dad, and Emma were watching the early evening news.

'And finally,' said the newscaster, 'an oak tree thought to be more than five hundred years old met its doom today, when it was cut down to make way for a new bypass.'

The screen showed footage of a huge tree swaying, while a chainsaw roared.

'The tree has a strange legend attached to it,' the newscaster continued. 'It's said to have been planted by a witch, who prophesied that if ever the tree should be destroyed, black rain will fall, and won't stop falling until the whole world is drowned.'

'Oh!' cried Emma nervously.

'But even an eerie legend can't stop progress,' said the newscaster. 'Work will begin on the bypass tomorrow. So let's go over to the weather forecast, and hope that it isn't going to rain, ha ha!'

Emma was very upset when the programme finished. 'What if the legend's true?' she said.

'Don't be silly,' Mum told her. 'It's just a tree.'

'But if it rains—'

'You heard what the weatherman said,' Dad put in.

'It's going to be sunny all week. Stop worrying, and finish your tea.'

Next morning it *was* sunny, and Emma had forgotten all about the oak tree. Mum did a load of washing and hung it in the garden. It was Saturday, so Emma didn't have to go to school. She was playing computer games in her room when suddenly Mum shouted up the stairs.

'Emma! It's started raining—come and help me get the washing in, quickly!'

Emma ran downstairs and out into the garden. The rain had only just started, but it was already teeming down. She grabbed a sheet off the washing line, reached for another—and stopped.

The rain was soaking the sheet. And turning it black.

Foot and Mouth

An unpleasant couple from the city had gone to the country for a relaxing day out. In the morning they went to the village shop, and were rude to the shopkeeper when she didn't have what they wanted. At lunchtime they went to a pub, and were rude to the landlord when he didn't serve the sort of food they liked. Then in the afternoon they went for a walk over the farmland. They dropped litter, left gates open, and trampled on crops. They weren't bothered. Someone else could clear up their mess.

After a while they came to a gate with a notice pinned to it. The notice said:

DANGER.
FOOT AND MOUTH.
KEEP OUT!

'What's Foot and Mouth?' she asked.

'It's some sort of disease,' he said. 'But we needn't worry. People can't catch it, only animals. Come on.'

They opened the gate, but before they could walk through, a voice called, 'Hey! What d'you think you're doing?'

A boy was running towards them, waving. 'Can't you read?' he demanded. 'It says, KEEP OUT!'

'Don't be stupid,' sneered the man. 'We're humans, not sheep. Humans don't get Foot and Mouth.'

'But—' the boy began.

'Go away,' the woman interrupted. 'Go on. Mind your own business and stop bothering us!'

Before the boy could say another word, they went through the gate—leaving it open—and walked away, while the boy stared after them with his mouth like a wide 'O'.

'Stupid kid!' the man said. 'What does he know about anything?'

'He's just an ignorant country bumpkin,' said the woman smugly. '*We're* from the city. City people are more intelligent.'

'That's right. He'll probably never even go to college!'

They strolled happily on across the field. Until, out of the sky, a gigantic foot came slamming down, and squashed the woman flat.

And at the same moment, an enormous mouth opened up in the ground, and swallowed the man whole.

From the gate the boy still stared. Well, he'd *tried* to warn them, hadn't he? It wasn't his fault if they wouldn't listen.

Stupid townies.

He closed the gate, and went home.

The Lighthouse

'*Tonight!*' cried the wind.

'*Tonight!*' screamed the gulls.

And the surging waves of the sea seemed to whisper, '*Tonight . . . tonight . . . tonight . . .*'

The sun set fiery red, and the moon rose cool and white. The lighthouse beam shone out into the dark, revolving and revolving. *Flash. Flash. Flash.*

The old woman sat at her window in the house by the harbour. She heard the wind, and she saw the moon, and she watched the *flash . . . flash . . . flash . . .* of the lighthouse. She felt happy. For the wind, and the gulls, and the sea, had told her that, tonight, her son would return. His ship had been away for so long, but now at last it was coming home.

Flash. Flash. Flash. Then in the turning beam of the lighthouse she saw the ship. Slowly and gracefully it came in, sails silver in the moonlight. And then there was laughter on the quay, people bustling, ropes being made fast. She waited breathlessly for the gangplank to be let down, and she peered as hard as she could, eager for her first glimpse of her sailor boy.

There he was! Tall and strong, with his sea-chest on his shoulder, striding from the quay towards the little house and the mother who had waited for so long. She heard his footsteps approaching. She heard the front door opening. She ran to greet him in the hall, crying, 'My dearest son, you have come back to me at last!'

The sailor looked around him. *Flash. Flash. Flash.* The lighthouse beam shone in to the familiar, welcoming room. He smiled, a little sadly but with pleasure, too. It was good to be on land again. It was good to be *home*.

He put his sea-chest on the floor, and he poured himself a small tot of rum, and he sat down in his favourite chair, by the window.

Flash. Flash. Flash. The lighthouse shone on the sailor's brown and weatherbeaten face as he dozed in his chair. And, unseen, unheard, the old woman's ghost faded into the darkness between the flashes, and was gone.

Big Ones

I t isn't fun waking up in the middle of the night, in the dark.

It's even less fun when you wake up, and you hear voices whispering, and you know there shouldn't be anybody else there.

That's what happened to Danny. Wide awake. In the dark. *Whisper, whisper.* Low voices. Deep voices. *Huge* voices.

Then he heard what they were whispering.

The first voice said: 'I think we should eat him now.'

Danny's hair stood on end.

The second voice said: 'No! I vote we save him for later.'

Danny started to shake.

'Eat him now!' snarl-whispered the first voice.

'Save him for later!' growl-whispered the second voice.

Danny's eyes were starting to get used to the dark, and for the first time he saw what was in his room. Or rather, he saw their shapes. Two hunched, bulging shapes, silhouetted against his window. They were huge. Oh, they were *huge*. Their heads touched the ceiling.

Their shoulders were almost as wide as the whole room. They could swallow him up in one mouthful each. One would swallow his head and body, the other would swallow his hips and legs. Danny felt as if he was half-eaten already.

'Now!' argued the first.

'Later!' insisted the second.

The first voice grumbled and rumbled, like a thunderstorm coming from a very long way off. 'No!' it said. 'We've *got* to eat him now. Because if we don't, the *big* ones will come and take him away from us!'

Hide and Seek

There was a big party at the manor house when Cedric and Emily, the Squire's twins, celebrated their birthday. After tea, the children all played hide-and-seek.

'I'm going to hide up a tree by the lake,' said Cedric.

'I'm not allowed to climb trees,' Emily grumbled. 'Where can I hide?'

'How about the big oak chest at the end of the landing, where no one ever goes?' Cedric suggested. 'You get in, and I'll shut the lid down. No one'll *ever* find you.'

She looked doubtful. 'But the lid's too heavy for me to open by myself. What if I get stuck in there?'

'You won't,' said Cedric. 'At the end of the game I'll let you out. Promise.' He grinned. 'You're sure to win!'

Emily trusted her brother. 'All right,' she said.

The Squire started to count to one hundred and the children ran off to hide. Cedric helped Emily into the oak chest, then raced to the lake and climbed the tallest willow tree. Higher he went, until he was hidden among the leaves. The branch began to sway. He heard an ominous creak . . .

The branch broke. Cedric hit his head as he fell, and he was unconscious when he splashed into the lake.

Soon all the children had been found, except for Cedric and Emily. The Squire and his wife were worried; a search was ordered, and as the sun set they found Cedric's body in the lake.

And upstairs, at the end of the landing where no one ever went, Emily banged on the lid of the chest and cried, 'Help! Oh, please help me!'

But there was nobody to hear her.

Cedric's funeral was very sad and solemn, and everyone sobbed as the small coffin was carried into the church. Such a shame, they all said, that Emily had not been found. Obviously she had climbed the tree with her brother, and they had both fallen into the lake. She must be lying down there among the weeds, they whispered. Such a tragedy . . .

The Squire and his wife could not bear to stay in the manor. They and their servants went away that night, leaving the house shuttered and empty.

And on the landing where no one had thought to go, Emily scratched, feebly now, on the lid of the oak chest and whispered, '*Help . . . me . . .* '

But there was nobody to hear her.

Emergency Landing

'Ladies and gentlemen, this is your captain speaking,' said the voice over the intercom. 'I'm afraid we have engine trouble, so we'll have to make an emergency landing. There's no cause for alarm; we can get down quite safely. I apologize for the inconvenience.'

'Bother!' said one of the passengers. 'I've got an important meeting, and I don't want to be late.'

'Where are we, anyway?' said the passenger in the seat next to him. They both peered out of the porthole. 'I suppose we'll land down there,' said the first passenger. 'It looks like the only possible place. I don't recognize it, though.'

The stewardess, who was coming down the aisle, overheard. 'It is rather in the middle of nowhere, I'm afraid,' she said ruefully. 'We won't find a qualified mechanic there. But don't worry; the crew have been trained to do repairs, and they shouldn't take very long.'

'Hmm. Will we be able to make ourselves understood to the natives?' the first passenger asked.

'I shouldn't think so, sir. I shouldn't think anyone there can speak our language.'

The passengers didn't like the sound of that. 'What if they're hostile?' someone else wanted to know. 'We could be in danger!'

The stewardess laughed. Or rather, she waggled four of her six antennae, which amounted to the same thing. 'Don't worry,' she chuckled. 'We've got weapons that no one there has even *dreamed* of! So if there's any trouble, we just power them up and—*pffft!*'

They all looked out of the portholes at the little blue-and-green world revolving against a background of deep-space stars. The people who lived on the little world called it Earth, though the passengers didn't know that, and wouldn't have cared if they had.

'I expect,' said the stewardess comfortably, 'we'll blow the planet up when we leave. We usually do.' She waggled her antennae again. 'It saves a lot of silly form-filling and questions when we get home. Now, ladies and gentlemen; if you would kindly fasten your seat belts as we go in to land . . . '

Sticky Ending (2)

Lights gone out.
Leaking gas.
Strike a match.
Silly ass.

Sticky Ending (3)

Hairpin bend.
Speeding truck.
Brakes don't work.
Oh. Bad luck.

Teeth

When one of her milk teeth fell out, Mum said, 'Put it under your pillow tonight, and while you're asleep the Tooth Fairy will come and give you 20p.'

In the morning the tooth was gone, and there was 20p, just like Mum had promised. Not bad.

The next tooth that fell out was bigger, and she thought it ought to be worth more. You couldn't do much with 20p. 50p was more like it. Or even a pound.

But there was only 20p under her pillow in the morning. It wasn't fair. The Tooth Fairy was *mean*.

When the third tooth came out, she wrote a note. *'Dear Tooth Fairy,'* it said. *'20p isn't enough. I want one pound. Or even two.'*

In the morning, she looked eagerly under her pillow. The note had gone. And there was 20p.

She was very cross, so she decided on a plan.

Out came another tooth, and under her pillow it went. But this time she only pretended to be asleep. At midnight, a teeny creature appeared. It had gossamer wings, and it was carrying a teeny bag. It felt under the pillow with a teeny hand, and—

22

'*Gotcha!*' she cried. The Tooth Fairy squealed and wriggled, but she didn't let go. 'Didn't you get my note?' she demanded. 'I want more money for my teeth!'

'It's not allowed!' gasped the Tooth Fairy. 'Rules are rules—20p per tooth!'

'I want more!' she growled. 'If you don't give it to me, I'll *squash* you!' She squeezed, to show what she meant.

'Look,' spluttered the fairy, 'I'm only doing my job! I can't give you more money unless you give me more teeth! Two pounds, at 20p a tooth—that's . . . ten teeth!'

'All right,' she said. 'Come back tomorrow night. And make sure you've got money with you, *or else.*'

That night, she took Grandad's dentures from the bathroom. Loads of teeth there—she'd get *at least* two pounds! She put the dentures under her pillow and went to sleep feeling pleased with herself.

In the morning she stuck her hand under the pillow—'OWWWW! OH, HELP! MUM!'

The dentures had snapped shut on her fingers, and they wouldn't come off. Grandad found a two-pound coin under his pillow. He never worked out where it came from. She had to go to hospital to have the dentures removed. Her fingers hurt for weeks. And under *her* pillow there was a note, in teeny writing.

'*That'll teach you,*' it said.

It did.

Blood Relations

D o you believe in vampires?

The old people of my mountain village believed in them. Grandmother did; and when my older sister and I scoffed, she would say we were foolish girls who should listen to their elders. But we laughed at her silly superstitions.

Until my sister met Vasili.

Vasili was new to our district. He was dark and handsome, and all the girls fell for him. When he courted my sister, her friends were madly jealous. But I was suspicious. Vasili's face was *so* pale, and his hair *so* black. He only came to our house after dark. He never ate or drank in front of us. And my sister was pale, too, and tired all the time . . . It fitted, horribly, with Grandmother's frightening stories.

My sister just laughed at my fears. But I was afraid. What if Vasili *was* a vampire? She could be in terrible danger.

So one winter day, after school, I went to Vasili's house. There wasn't much daylight left when I arrived. But I had to know the truth.

I knocked. There was no reply. Screwing up my

courage, I tried the door. It creaked open, and I tiptoed in.

My blood ran cold. A coffin stood in the middle of the floor. Its lid was closed, and all I wanted was to run away, to the safety of home. But I thought of my sister. And I clutched the hammer and the wooden stake that I had brought with me . . .

I lifted the lid, and there he was. Vasili, fast asleep, with a cruel smile on his face. And blood on his mouth.

I poised the stake over his heart. I raised the hammer. I shut my eyes and the hammer came down—

His scream was the most hideous sound I had ever heard. But when I dared to open my eyes again, he was *truly* dead.

At that moment the sun vanished behind the mountains. I heard a sound behind me. I whirled round, and there was my sister. I was so thankful; I ran to her—and my joy turned to horror as she opened her mouth in a snarl, and I saw her long, long teeth—

So now we live here together, my sister and I. No one believes in us. Well, it's been a hundred years, and people aren't superstitious any more. Tourists come to our village now. Maybe *you'll* come for a holiday one day. *Do* you believe in vampires?

I think you should. I really do.

Cheers

'Come on,' said Dave Lex. 'I'm all right. I'll drive home.'

Sally Fielding knew he was drunk. They'd been at the pub all evening, and they were both way over the drink-driving limit. But there weren't many police cars around at this time of night. They wouldn't get caught.

They swayed towards the car, then Dave said, 'I've got to go to the loo.' He gave her the keys. 'Get in. I won't be a minute.'

He tottered back into the pub. Sally was about to unlock the car when a shadow moved under the street lamp. An older man was walking slowly past, limping with the aid of a stick. As the lamp lit his face, she recoiled—he had terrible scars. And his eyes were hauntingly sad.

He said: 'Good evening.'

'G-good evening.' Sally didn't want to talk to him, but she couldn't be rude and ignore him. He stopped, staring at the car, and she began to feel uneasy.

Then he said, 'I drove home when I was drunk, once.'

'Oh,' she said. 'Right.' *Hurry up, Dave! This guy's giving me the creeps!*

26

'I crashed the car,' said the man quietly. 'They said I was lucky to survive.' He looked down at himself. 'But it ruined my life.'

'Oh,' Sally repeated. She couldn't think of anything else to say.

'My girlfriend died,' the man went on. 'I can never forget. I killed her. I loved her, and I killed her because I insisted on driving her home that night.'

'I'm . . . um . . . sorry,' Sally mumbled. *I don't want to hear your stories! Go away!*

'I'm sorry, too,' said the man. 'But at least I'm alive. She isn't. And it was all my fault.' He sighed. 'My poor, darling Sally . . . '

Sally's blood ran cold. The man started to limp on, and suddenly she called out to him in a shrill, nervous voice. 'Wait!' He looked back at her and she added, 'Wh . . . what's your name?'

'Dave,' said the man. 'Dave Lex.'

When she looked again, there was nobody there.

Sally heard footsteps, and saw Dave coming back from the loo. Her heart pounded; her fist closed round the car keys. There was a drain a couple of metres away. She dropped the keys down the drain.

'Hey!' said Dave. 'What—'

'Come on,' she said, hoping he couldn't see how white her face was. 'We're walking home.'

Who's There?

The door slammed, shutting him in. When he tried to open it, he found it was locked. There was no window, no light. He couldn't see anything at all. And he couldn't get out, unless someone came to help him.

Quaveringly, he called, 'Help! Is anybody there?'

And a deep, echoing voice said:—'NO.'

Till Death Us Do Part

'No!' said the miser to his daughter. 'I forbid you to marry young Jack! You must wed Ephraim the merchant!'

'But Ephraim is old and ugly!' she cried.

'And *rich*,' said the miser, rubbing his hands together. 'I shall have five purses of gold for your dowry!'

She pleaded and wept, but her father was adamant. Jack was only an apothecary's son. She must marry Ephraim. He had a pockmarked face, no teeth, and a hunched back. But in those days, children did not disobey their fathers.

' . . . Till death do you part,' droned the parson as Ephraim put the wedding ring on her finger.

And that was when she had the idea.

They went back to Ephraim's fine house. Pretending to be happy, she poured Ephraim a large glass of brandy. Before long he fell asleep in his chair, and she slipped out of the house to find Jack.

When she told him what she wanted, Jack was surprised. But he was an apothecary's son, so he knew about such things. She returned to Ephraim's house with a small bag of herbs.

On the following night, she put the herbs into his brandy glass.

Ephraim's death looked like natural causes. A heart seizure, no doubt. He was very old, after all. The girl's father had his five bags of gold, so he did not mind.

And the girl was a rich widow.

She and Jack got married, and soon they were sitting together by candlelight in their house, which not long ago had been Ephraim's.

'A toast,' said Jack, pouring wine. 'To us, my dearest!'

'To us!' she cried. They drank. 'At last, my love! I have longed for this day, and—*uhh!*'

She clamped a hand to her throat. There was something wrong with the wine! She couldn't breathe; the room was spinning round; she felt sick—

'Jack!' she croaked. 'I am ill!'

'Not ill, my dear,' said Jack, and his cruel smile struck horror in her heart. 'You are *dying*. I have poisoned you.' He laughed. 'You gave me the idea when you asked me for those herbs to kill old Ephraim. I don't love you. I never did. But you're rich, and I *do* love money!'

There was a roaring in her ears. The world was going dark. She collapsed to the floor, twitched, then was still. Jack looked down at her.

'How sad,' he said. 'I'm a wealthy widower now.'

Monsters

Robbie's little brother, Pete, was scared of going to sleep.

'There's a monster under my bed!' he wailed. 'As soon as I'm asleep it'll creep out and eat me!'

'Don't be so stupid,' said Mum. 'There's no monster.' She stuck a broom handle under the bed and waggled it. 'See? Nothing!'

'It's hiding!' insisted Pete. 'It'll come back!'

Mum got cross, but Robbie was kinder.

'Don't worry,' he told Pete. 'I used to think there was a monster under my bed, too. I was really scared, till I got rid of it.'

Pete looked hopeful. 'How?' he asked.

'Easy,' said Robbie. 'I waited till I heard it moving around, then I hung over the side of the bed and shone a torch straight at it.'

'Wow!' Pete's eyes widened. 'What did you see?'

Robbie grinned. 'Nothing. There wasn't any monster, and once I knew that, I was never scared again.' He held out his own torch. 'Here you are. Try it tonight, and see if it works.'

Pete was much happier when he went to bed that

night. When Mum turned his light off he settled down with Robbie's torch, waiting for the monster. It wasn't long before he heard it. *Scrabble, scrabble . . . scritch-scratch . . .* Like claws scraping on the floor. Then a sort of . . . *heaving* noise.

'There isn't any monster, there isn't any monster,' Pete whispered over and over to himself. He leaned over the edge of the bed and switched on the torch, shining it straight at the spot where the monster ought to be.

He didn't even have time to scream. It only took one gulp, and there was no more Pete.

Outside the bedroom door, Robbie grinned. *Dumb kid*, he thought. *They always fall for it. His big brother did, too.*

He went into the room, and changed himself into his *real* shape. The other monster was squatting on the floor. 'Hi,' it said, and burped, licking its lips.

'Hi,' said the monster who had looked like Robbie. 'You'd better turn yourself into Pete. Be quick, in case one of the grown-up humans comes in.'

'Oh. Right,' said the monster. It changed, and when it looked like Pete, it got into bed.

'Boys?' came Mum's voice from downstairs. 'Time you were asleep!'

'OK, Mum!' Robbie called. He grinned. The other monster grinned.

'Their turn next,' he said.

Midsummer Night

'Do you know,' said Carly, 'there's a legend that if you go to the churchyard at midnight on Midsummer Night, you'll see all the people who are going to die round here in the next year going in at the door. Why don't we try it, tonight?'

Linda thought it was a great idea, but Amy wasn't keen. 'The churchyard's spooky,' she said. 'I'd be scared.'

The others tried to talk her into it. There wasn't much to do in a small village; this would be a laugh. At last Amy gave in, so at half-past eleven the three friends crouched by the churchyard wall. It was eerily quiet. A full moon shone through the trees, casting uneasy shadows. Then, loud in the night silence, the church clock struck twelve.

'Look!' Linda hissed. 'There—going in at the gate!'

A shadowy figure drifted past them.

'It's old Mrs Goddard,' said Carly.

'Well, she's over ninety. If she dies, it won't be a surprise,' Linda whispered. 'Oh! There's another! Joe Blake—he's seriously ill, isn't he?'

Amy started to shiver. She didn't want to believe this was happening. Carly and Linda were shocked, too. They hadn't taken the legend seriously. They'd just thought it would be a bit of fun, and they certainly hadn't expected to see anything like this!

Then three more ghostly shapes appeared. Two men, and a girl.

Carly frowned. 'Who are they? I don't know them . . . '

'Neither do I,' murmured Linda. Then her eyes widened. 'But the girl! It's—'

'It's *me*!' Amy cried in horror. At the same moment a far-off, screeching wail echoed out of the night. Amy started to scream.

'It's me, it's me! I can hear the ghosts—I'm going to die!'

Panicking, she ran away towards the road.

'Amy, come back!' Linda shouted. 'It isn't ghosts, it's a siren!'

The stolen van, with the police car in pursuit, came hurtling round a bend as Amy ran across the road. The two men in the van were killed when it swerved and smashed into the wall. And Amy didn't stand a chance.

Carly and Linda were too upset to go to Amy's funeral. But they saw the pictures of the two dead men in the local paper. They had seen them before. In the churchyard. With Amy.

They would never laugh at legends again.

Moving House

I shouldn't have done it. I really shouldn't. But it's too late to be sorry now.

Mum and Dad had decided to move home, so I went along with them to look at a house. It was an old house, and it hadn't been lived in for a while. I liked it, especially when I saw that it had a cellar. Well, there was this door under the stairs—it had to lead to a cellar, didn't it? But when I tried to open it, it was locked.

'Oh,' said the estate agent, 'there's no cellar. It was filled in. The door's sealed up, and there's just solid brick behind it.'

He took Mum and Dad into the kitchen. But I stayed behind. That door looked so *interesting*. I was certain there must be *something* behind it.

Then I saw a rusty key hanging by the door. And sure enough, when I tried it in the cellar door, it fitted. The door wasn't sealed up at all. As soon as I turned the key it creaked open, and behind it . . . *Yes!* There was a flight of steps vanishing into darkness. Of course, I went down them. Down and down. They seemed to go on forever. And they kept turning and twisting, until I was . . .

Lost.

Oh, yes; lost. Because when I turned round, there were the steps behind me. Only they led *downwards*, not back up. I looked for steps that went up, but there weren't any.

'Mum?' I called. 'Dad?'

No one answered.

'Help!' I shouted.

But no help came.

I don't know how long I've been down here. It must be ages, because I'm much taller, and I've got a long beard. My clothes don't fit me now, but I can't get any more. I have food, though, because there are lots of rats and spiders here. And when it rains outside—wherever 'outside' is—water trickles down the walls, so I get enough to drink. But I wish someone would come. They must have tried to find me. Why haven't they? Maybe the steps have got something to do with it. Because whichever direction I turn, there they are. Always leading *down*.

So if you ever find a key to a door that people say can't be opened because there's nothing there . . .

Well, don't pick that key up. Just *don't*. Right?

The Storm

The father heard the hissing sound high overhead. He looked up, and to his horror saw the boiling mass of clouds sweeping across the sky towards them.

'Mother!' he cried. 'The rain! The rain!'

The mother saw, and screamed. 'Help the children!' she wailed. 'We must save the children!'

Other families had heard the noise and seen the clouds now, and panic broke out in the community as all the parents rushed to gather their children together. But there were so many children, and so many different places for them to play.

'We'll never find them all in time!' the mother sobbed. 'Oh, hurry, hurry!'

The sky darkened and the hissing grew louder, until it became a thundering roar. 'Save them, save them!' cried the mother.

'It's too late!' shouted someone else. 'The storm's almost on us—save yourself, if you can!'

Then the rain began. It was a drenching downpour, hot and stinging and choking. Everyone scattered, desperately trying to reach shelter. But there was no shelter from that rain. Screams rang out above the roaring in the sky. Bodies fell, struck down by the deadly storm. The father tried to drag the mother to safety as the rain hammered down on them. He heard her cry out, saw her collapse. And he was coughing, choking, half drowned and half poisoned. The world blurred. The screams faded. And he fell, to lie dead with her, among the bodies of their children and their neighbours as, at last, the clouds moved on and the rain stopped.

The gardener switched off his insecticide sprayer. He looked at the rose bush and grunted with satisfaction.

'Pesky greenfly!' he said to himself. 'That's got rid of them!'

He stumped away, leaving the rose bush dripping in the summer sunshine.

Gold

'**I** love gold!' said the greedy king. 'Bring me gold!'
His ministers brought him all the gold they could find. But it wasn't enough.

'I want more!' cried the king. 'More gold! Now!'

The ministers ordered that everyone in the kingdom must give up all the gold they had, and bring it to the king. Soon, the throne room was filled with gold.

'It still isn't enough!' the king roared. 'More, more! I *love* gold!'

'But there's no more gold anywhere in the kingdom,' the ministers wailed.

'I want more!' screamed the king. 'Send for the court wizard!'

The court wizard came. 'Cast a spell so that everything I touch turns into gold!' the king commanded.

'Yes, Sire,' said the wizard. 'But if I cast such a spell, remember that only I can undo it.'

'Yes, yes,' snapped the king impatiently. 'Do it! *Now!*'

The wizard cast the spell. When it was completed, the king sat down on his throne—and the throne turned to solid gold. Cackling with delight, the king ran around the palace, touching everything he could find.

Furniture, tapestries, portraits of his ancestors; they all turned into gold.

'Now I am happy!' he crowed. 'I shall hold a banquet to celebrate!'

The servants rushed around to prepare the feast, while the king sat gloating on his solid gold throne. The first dish was served. The king picked up his knife and fork, which turned to gold. He bit on a mouthful of roast peacock—

The food turned to gold as it touched his lips.

'No!' he wailed. 'Not my food! I must eat, or I'll starve to death! Fetch the court wizard, quickly!'

The court wizard came hurrying.

'Help me!' begged the king. 'I don't want the spell any more—take it away!'

In his fear and anguish he reached out and caught hold of the wizard's sleeve.

And the wizard, who was the only one who could undo the spell, turned into a solid gold statue.

Come Back!

I was on holiday in Scotland. I'd been walking on a windswept moor, and I was heading back to the village in the dusk when I heard a voice calling.

'Come back! Dougie, where are you? Oh, come back!'

A woman came running through the heather. She was very distressed. When she saw me, she came stumbling in my direction.

'Have you seen him?' she gasped.

'Seen who?' I asked in confusion.

'My little boy—my Dougie!' She was crazed with worry. 'He strayed away from me, and I've lost him!'

'That's terrible!' I said. 'Have you told the police?'

She looked at me strangely and didn't answer.

'They'll organize a search,' I went on. 'I'll go to the village and contact them for you!'

Again, that strange look. Then suddenly she gave an awful, broken laugh—a crazed laugh—and ran off.

'Wait!' I shouted. But she took no notice. She just kept running, and as she ran I heard her voice: 'Dougie! Come back!' Then she vanished into the dusk.

I hurried back towards the village. Near the edge of the moor, I saw a pile of stones—a cairn, it's called—

beside the track. An old man was standing there, with a car nearby, and I hurried up to him.

'Can you drive me to the police station?' I asked. 'There's a little boy gone missing!'

'A little boy, you say?'

'Yes. I just saw his mother—she was running on the moor, looking for him. She's half-mad with worry!'

'Och,' he said, 'that would be Morag MacIlvor.'

'You know her?'

'I did. But Morag's been dead these seventy years.' His eyes filled with sadness. 'Her ghost haunts the moor. Many people have seen her. She could not find her child, and she thought he was dead. So in her grief she killed herself. She is buried here, beneath this cairn.'

'A . . . a *ghost?*' I echoed, stunned.

'Aye,' said the old man sadly.

'And the child . . . was he ever found?'

'He was. Safe and well. It was just a piece of mischief for him. But he came home too late to save his mother.' He gazed at the cairn and sighed.

'You seem to know a lot about the story,' I said uneasily.

'So I should,' replied the old man. 'You see . . . my name is Dougie MacIlvor.'

Do You Believe in Fairies?

Two children were playing under an apple tree.

'Do you believe in fairies?' asked one.

The other child shook his head and opened his mouth to say, 'No.'

But before he could speak, the first child cried, 'Don't! You've got to say you *do* believe, cos every time someone says they don't, a fairy dies!'

'Oh!' said the other child. 'All right, then.' And he added in a loud voice, 'I believe in fairies!'

Up in a high branch of the apple tree, two fairies breathed a sigh of relief.

'That was close!' said one.

'It was,' agreed the other, and looked thoughtful. 'I wonder if it works the other way round?'

'What do you mean?' The first fairy was curious.

'Let's try it,' said the other fairy. And in a voice too tiny for the children to hear, she said: 'I don't believe in children!'

One child gave a choking gasp and dropped dead in the grass.

The fairies grinned evilly. 'This is going to be *fun!*' they said.

Swapsies

I hate my baby brother.

Ever since Mum brought him home from hospital, she and Dad haven't had any time for me. It's all 'Look at the baby', 'Let's play with the baby', and 'Not now, we're looking after the baby'. They think he's sweet. But all he does is yell and throw up and have to have his nappy changed every five minutes. I *hate* him.

So I'm going to get rid of him.

I've worked out how to do it. I got the idea from a story in the fairy book Nan gave me for my birthday. In the story, this couple find a fairy ring—you know, a place where toadstools grow in a circle in the grass— and they dance there. That makes the fairies angry, so they steal the couple's baby and put a fairy child in its place. The parents never know what's happened. Well, I know where there's a fairy ring. And I'm going to go and dance there. A fairy child would be much more fun than my horrible baby brother.

I'm at the fairy ring now. I'm dancing. There's no one here to see me. I've made up a song, asking the fairies to come and take my brother away. Right. That's done. All I've got to do is wait.

Now I'm in bed. It's very late but I'm not sleepy. I'm listening for the fairies. I'm sure they'll come. And in the morning, no more baby brother.

There's a whispering noise on the landing. And I can see strange, flickering little lights under my door. *Yes!* They're here, whoopee! They'll tiptoe to the nursery, and—

Wait a minute. My door's opening. A crowd of tiny people are coming into my room. They've got wings. They're scowling at me. They look *furious*. No—no, hang on; it's *him* you want! Let go of my arms! Ow! Help! You're not supposed to do this, there's been a terrible mistake! You're supposed to take my brother!

Not *ME*!

Sticky Ending (4)

Crumbling cliff.
Sign: KEEP CLEAR.
Rumble, rumble . . .
CRASH! Oh dear.

Sticky Ending (5)

On a bike.
Doing tricks.
'Mind that wall—!'
Pile of bricks.

When the Aliens Came

I won't be able to outrun them for long. They're too clever.
They always are. Lots of people try to escape, and some
succeed. But we always get recaptured in the end.

*It's been like this ever since the aliens came. They arrived
in their spaceships like an invading army, and there was nothing
anyone could do. They've taken over the whole of the Earth
now. They're not cruel to us—they give us food and shelter.
But sometimes people get taken away, and are never seen again.
We don't know why, and we can't ask, because we don't
understand their language and they don't understand ours. We
don't know what they want with us . . .*

The aliens caught him soon enough. There was
nowhere he could hide from them; as he said, they were
too clever. They didn't punish him. Instead, they took
him back to the big, communal place where they kept
so many human beings. It was a nice place, and
everyone was well fed and no one had to work. But
why were they *there*?

The two aliens who took him back were talking,
and if he had been able to understand their speech, he
would have had his answer.

'They're very foolish,' said one, pityingly. 'I don't
understand why they keep trying to run away.'

'They're only animals,' said the other. 'They don't know any better. We'll put him back in his stall, but we'd better not let him have the free run of the farm again until he calms down.'

'Mmm.' The first alien looked at their captive. 'He's a bit young, isn't he? Not ready yet.'

'No, not yet. He needs to grow a bit bigger, get some real meat on him. Then we can move him to the fattening pens and feed him up. He'll probably be just right for our next big festival.'

Being aliens, they didn't lick their lips as humans might have done. But, like humans, they needed food, and they enjoyed eating *good* food. The food they had found on this planet was excellent.

After a hard day's chase, they were both looking forward to their evening meal.

Vanishing Lane

'Come on,' said my friend Bill. 'We're late. Let's take the short cut down Vanishing Lane.'

'No way!' I argued. 'I'm not walking along there after dark!'

'Whyever not?' asked my other friend, Sam.

I stared at them both. 'You know why it's called Vanishing Lane, don't you? Because people have *vanished* there!'

They both laughed at me. 'No one's vanished!' scoffed Bill, and Sam added, 'That's just a dumb story!'

'What about Glenda Brown, then?' I said. 'She disappeared, didn't she? So did old Joe Pike!'

'Who said they went anywhere near Vanishing Lane?' Sam demanded. 'If you ask me, Glenda ran off with some bloke, and old Joe got drunk again and still can't remember where he lives. Come on, Derek; let's get going!'

I was outnumbered, so we took the short cut down Vanishing Lane. It was very dark. You couldn't see any street lights, and the hedges loomed high, their branches like threatening fingers.

'You've got to admit it's creepy,' I said as we walked.

'Anywhere's creepy when there's no light at all,' said Bill. 'Isn't that right, Sam?' He paused. 'Sam . . . ?'

But Sam didn't answer. And now, I could only hear two sets of footsteps.

'Sam!' we shouted. 'Sam, stop messing around!'

But still there was no answer. Sam had just . . . gone.

'Where is he?' whispered Bill.

'I d–don't know,' I stammered. 'But I don't want to hang around!'

We started to walk faster. Then suddenly I could only hear one set of footsteps. Mine.

'Bill?' I called. 'Bill!'

There was no reply. Bill wasn't there. I was on my own.

I'm running as fast as I can now, and I'm so scared that I feel sick. I won't be safe till I reach the end of Vanishing Lane. It can't be much further! Please God, just let me get there before I v—

History Lesson

George's class were on a school trip to an ancient castle. A guide showed them round, but George was bored by her dry history lesson, so he wandered off on his own.

Soon, he found himself in a long gallery. There were suits of armour there, and shields, swords, and halberds fixed on the walls. And an axe. An *enormous* axe. George looked closely at it. The blade had chips out of it, and there were dark, brownish stains at the edge.

'Wow!' George said under his breath. 'I bet that's seen some action!'

'It certainly has,' said a voice behind him.

George jumped, and turned round to see a man standing there. The man smiled.

'Hello,' he said. 'Are you interested in history?'

'Not really,' George admitted. 'But I like battles and things. Was this axe used in battle?'

'Oh, no,' said the man. 'For something much more gruesome. It was an executioner's axe. And if you look out of the window, you'll see the block where people were beheaded centuries ago.'

George looked. 'Wow!' he said again, then glanced at the man with interest. 'Do you work here?'

'Yes,' said the man.

'So you know all about the castle's history?'

'Oh, yes. It's part of my job.'

'Great!' George enthused. 'Tell me about some of the executions!'

The man opened his mouth to start, but suddenly George heard his teacher calling.

'George! Come here at once! You're not allowed to wander off on your own!'

George pulled a face. 'I'd better go,' he said.

'Another time, then,' said the man pleasantly. 'Nice to have met you.'

He smiled. Then he removed his own head, tucked it under his arm, and walked away through the wall.

The Bride

The man I love got married today.

I went to the church. I know I shouldn't have done, but I couldn't stop myself. No one saw me go in. I stood at the back, away from the wedding guests, and I watched and listened as my beloved and his bride made their vows. My heart was breaking. But what could I do? What could I say? He has chosen her, and I don't suppose he even remembers me now.

The bells rang a joyful peal, and my love and his new wife walked down the aisle together and out into the bright sunshine. People threw confetti and took photographs. Then everyone waved as they drove away in a big car adorned with white ribbons.

The guests are all leaving for the reception now. And I must return to my grave, in the shadow of the churchyard wall . . .

Off With Her Head!

K ing Hubert was a happy king, except for one thing. His wife.

The Queen nagged. Oh, did she *nag*. Day and night: 'Do this, Hubert!' 'Don't do that, Hubert!' 'Hubert if I have to tell you one more time . . . '

After twenty years, King Hubert had had enough. So he decreed that nagging the king was treason. And treason, of course, is punishable by death.

The Queen nagged the guards as they marched her to the Execution Tower. She nagged the executioner as he tied her hands and made her kneel before the block. As the axe was raised, she looked up at King Hubert (who stood gloating) and said furiously, 'Hubert, stop this at once! I warn you—'

The axe came down on her neck with a THUCK! The Queen said, '*Urgh!*' and her severed head rolled on the ground. There was a *lot* of blood. And, at last, the Queen was silent.

King Hubert had the Queen's head put on a spike on the castle wall, as a warning to others. Then he threw a party, and did all the things the Queen used to tell him not to. He went to bed drunk, and dreamed happy dreams.

Until, in the small hours, a familiar voice said, 'Hubert! Wake up at once!'

King Hubert shot upright in bed.

'How *dare* you have me executed?' said the voice. 'I won't forget this, Hubert, and I'll make you suffer for it!'

Horrified, King Hubert ran on to his balcony. There in the moonlight he saw the spike, with the Queen's bloodstained head on it. And her mouth was moving.

'You can't still be nagging me!' cried Hubert. 'You're dead!'

'Ha!' snarled the Queen. 'You can't get rid of me that easily! I'm still here, Hubert. And no matter what you do, I always will be, until the day you die!'

King Hubert looked over the balcony to the ground. It was a long way down. A *very* long way.

He took a deep breath.

And jumped.

Revenge

From the upstairs window, we can see everything that happens in Josie's room. Josie's mum's putting her to bed. Soon, she'll be asleep. And then we'll carry out our plan.

Josie has a nightlight, because she's scared of the dark. That's great. It means we'll be able to see what we're doing. We've waited a long time for this, and now, at last, it's possible. All because Josie's mum left a package of sewing pins lying around by mistake . . .

Josie is a horrible little girl. She's got a real mean streak. We know that better than anyone, because she treats us worse than any of her so-called friends. She calls us names and tries to hurt us whenever she can. Well, now we're going to get our own back. Our mum and dad took a bit of persuading. They said if we did it, we'd be as bad as she is. But after what Josie did to Grandma, they changed their minds, and even agreed to help us. Our aunt and uncle are joining in, too. But not Grandad. He's gone to bed; he's probably still too upset.

Josie's mum is kissing her goodnight. Yuck. Who'd want to kiss Josie? Now she's turning the light off, so there's just the little glow of the nightlight. Josie'll be asleep in a few minutes. *Great.*

My older sister looks at me, and nods. Josie *is* asleep. We hurry downstairs, where Mum has taken all the sewing pins out of the packet. She gives us one each. They're very awkward to hold, but we can do it. There are ten of us altogether. Ten pins. They are going to *hurt*.

Dad's opening the front door. Lucky it doesn't creak. Lucky, too, that our house is on the ground at the moment. If it was up on the table, we'd have a real problem.

But even then, we'd manage somehow. Because we're so *angry* now. Especially about Grandma. I mean, you don't go around pulling people's heads off, do you? You just *don't*.

Tonight's the night, Josie. We're going to make you sorry for all the horrible things you've done to us for so long. Because even dolls in a dolls' house have feelings. And tonight, we're going to get our *revenge* . . .

The Wolf's Tale

You all know the story of Little Red Riding Hood, right? Well, I'm sure of one thing. You don't know what *really* happened. No one does, except me. I know people don't believe in fairy tales these days, but the Riding Hood story happens to be true. I should know. You see, I'm the wolf. And the rest of them—the girl, the woodsman, all the other people—they got it wrong. *All* wrong.

They think I killed and ate old Granny. I didn't. I wouldn't have harmed a hair of her head, but when I tried to tell them so, of course they couldn't understand me. So the woodsman cut me open. Oh, how that *hurt*. I can remember the pain; it was horrible. Even now I have nightmares about it, and I shudder and cry out in my sleep, until I wake up screaming.

They didn't kill me, you see. They thought they did, but they didn't. I can't be killed that way. It has to be something else. A silver bullet, that's the only thing that will work. A silver bullet, for a werewolf.

Because that's what I really am. I was attacked by a werewolf one night, years ago. It bit me, and infected me with its curse. I'd give anything to be free. I'd rather die than live like this, changing every full moon into a monster that no one can control. I'd give anything to be what I used to be. A harmless human being. A little old lady, who was kind to everyone.

Red Riding Hood thought she knew all about her dear granny.

But she didn't. No one does.

Only me . . . and, now, you.

Gimme!

'Gimme your sweets!' Jacko growled. He loomed menacingly over Peter, who was squashed in a corner of the school bike shed. 'I know you've got some—hand 'em over, or else!'

Peter was very small and weedy. He was a scaredy-cat, too, and that made him the perfect target for a big, bullying boy like Jacko. Nearly every morning Jacko cornered him when no one else was around, and took his sweets. Peter was too frightened to argue.

'Come on, I said *gimme*!' Jacko was getting impatient. Fumbling, Peter handed over all his sweets; even his last grubby peppermint. Jacko snatched them, stuffed them in his own pocket, then frowned threateningly. 'Right! Now get into class. And you know what'll happen if you tell, don't you?'

Peter gulped and nodded.

'Say it, then! Say what'll happen!'

Jacko loomed closer, and Peter stammered, 'S-something worse than the b-b-b-bogeyman'll get me . . . '

'Yeah! And who's worse than the bogeyman?'

'Y-y-you, Jacko,' Peter whispered.

'Right!' Jacko snarled. 'I'm more horrible than any

bogeyman there's ever been, and if you tell tales, I'll tear you in bits and stuff you in the dustbin! Got it?'

'G-g-got it, Jacko . . . I w-won't tell. Cross my heart!'

Peter scuttled out of the bike shed. He'd got off lightly. At least Jacko had only threatened him today. What a bully, Peter thought—he really was scarier than a bogeyman.

In the bike shed, Jacko grinned. He took Peter's choc bar out of his pocket and started to unwrap it.

Something reached out of the gloom and tapped him on the shoulder.

Jacko yelped and spun round. Then he said, '*Aargh!*'

Behind him stood a huge, bulging monster. It was covered in matted hair, and its arms were so long that its knuckles trailed on the ground. In its hideous face were piggy red eyes and a great, wide, grinning mouth full of yellow fangs.

'Hi,' it said in a voice that shook the whole shed. 'I'm the *real* bogeyman. And you owe me some sweets.'

It clamped one of its hairy hands round Jacko's throat, and held out the other, palm upwards. 'Gimme,' it said ominously. 'And if you ever tell . . . ' it cackled, then started to drool greedily. 'You *know* what'll happen. Don't you?'

Genie-us

'**I**f you want to marry my daughter,' said the king, 'you must prove yourself worthy of her hand.'

'Anything!' cried the poor young man. 'I love the princess, and I will brave any peril for her!'

The princess stood behind the throne, crying. 'Right then,' said the king. 'You must climb to the top of the Ice Mountain, and fetch the magic lamp that a wicked rival stole from me.'

'I'll do it!' the young man declared, and rushed from the throne room.

The king chuckled. 'That's fixed him! The cheek of it—poor as a church mouse, and weedy too, and he thinks he's good enough to marry my daughter! Well, *he* won't be back!'

The princess was still crying.

The young man might have been poor and weedy, but his love for the princess gave him courage. He struggled up the freezing, slippery slopes of the Ice Mountain. And he found the wicked rival's hideaway, where the magic lamp was hidden. (Luckily, the rival was away at the time.)

Holding the lamp, he wondered what sort of magic

it could do. You were supposed to rub magic lamps, weren't you? Well, then . . .

He rubbed the lamp. And—*WHOOSH!* A cloud of purple smoke burst out, and a genie appeared. The genie was tall and handsome and proud. He said, 'Who are you?'

'I'm a poor young man who loves the princess. And when I take the magic lamp, with you in it, back to the king, he'll let me marry her,' said the young man happily.

'In your dreams!' snorted the genie. He reached out and grabbed the young man. 'I've been in that lamp for a hundred years, and I'm fed up with it! So you can take my place—in you go!'

And with another puff of smoke, the young man vanished into the lamp.

The genie picked up the lamp, grabbed a magic carpet that was rolled up in a corner, and told it to take him to the palace.

'I've brought your lamp,' he announced as he strode into the throne room. 'It isn't magic any more. But I am. And I claim your daughter's hand in marriage!'

The king looked at the genie. Tall and handsome, and magic, too! 'That's more like it!' he said, and turned to the princess. 'Daughter, this is your future husband!'

The princess stopped crying. 'Oh, goody!' she said. 'I was so afraid I'd have to marry that poor, weedy creep instead!'

Wolf!

J an the goat-boy hated his job. All day he sat on
the hillside above the village, watching the goats.
The goats didn't do anything except eat grass.
And the bells round their necks went *clang-clonk-
tinkle* all the time, which got on Jan's nerves. He was
supposed to keep watch in case a wolf came. Not that
one ever had. But if one did, then he had to shout,
'Wolf! Wolf!' and blow the whistle the villagers had
given him.

One day Jan was so bored that he decided to give
the villagers a fright. Jumping to his feet, he shouted,
'Wolf! Wolf!' and blew the whistle as hard as he
could.

At once there was an uproar in the village. Jan
watched, grinning, as people came running out of their
houses, and men armed with sticks raced up the hill
towards him.

'Where's the wolf?' the men panted as they reached
him.

'It ran away when it saw you coming,' said Jan.

'Thank goodness!' said the men. But some of them
looked suspicious . . .

Jan thought the whole thing was fun, so a few days

later he did it again. Again, when the men came racing, he said the wolf had run away. This time, though, he sniggered, and the men realized that they had been tricked. Jan got a furious telling-off, and they warned him not to try that again, or else.

But Jan couldn't resist the temptation. It was so funny to see all the villagers panicking and running around, so he cried 'Wolf!' and blew his whistle a third time. The men were livid, and Jan's father gave him a thrashing. That hurt. Jan thought that perhaps he'd better stop playing practical jokes.

Three days later, he was watching the goats as usual when he heard a growl behind him. Jan turned—and there, large as life and twice as frightening, was a real wolf! It growled again, showing its fangs. It began to creep towards him . . .

'*Wolf!*' yelled Jan. '*Wolf, wolf! Help!*' The goats ran away, but Jan was too scared to move, though he blew the whistle until he turned purple. The wolf crept nearer. And down in the village, people said, 'That wretched boy's up to his tricks again. We're not fooled this time! We'll ignore him.'

They found the whistle on the hilltop next morning. But they didn't find anything else.

The Hounds

Take my advice, and don't go near Hunter's Moor after dark. It's a terrible place; bleak and grim. The wind howls over it like a lost soul. And as for how it got its name . . .

You haven't heard the story of the old Squire? He lived round here a hundred years ago, and he loved to hunt at break-neck speed across the moor, with his pack of hounds baying beside him. But he was a cruel man. He'd thrash his servants if they did anything to displease him. And woe betide any horse that stumbled with him on it, or any hound that didn't obey the call of his hunting horn.

Then one winter day the Squire was out hunting as usual. He had been chasing a fox all afternoon, but his horse and hounds were so tired that they couldn't run any further, so the fox got away. The Squire was furious. He sprang down from his horse, and he whipped the poor creature savagely. Then he turned on the hounds and began to beat them, too, shouting and ranting. At last, in a towering rage, he snatched up the pistols he always carried and shot the horse and the dogs, firing and firing until they were all dead.

As the last hound died, the Squire gave an agonized

cry, clutched his chest and fell to the ground. His rage had proved too much for his heart, and he was as dead as his poor animals.

So now, they say, the ghosts of the Squire and his horse and his dogs haunt Hunter's Moor. Many people round here say they've seen them: the Squire running in fear and desperation, pursued by a galloping horse that has no rider, and a pack of hounds baying for revenge. He can never outrun them. They will chase him over the moor for ever, and he will never be free. That's how Hunter's Moor got its name.

The sun's setting now. Soon it will be dark, and then I will hear the galloping hooves and the yelping, baying dogs. And I must run again. As I always will. As I always must.

So don't come near the moor. Stay away.

Or you might just see me running . . .

Search Party

'Goodbye, dearest,' said the prince to his wife. 'I'm going hunting in the Dark Wood. I'll be back in about two days.'

He and all the men of the castle rode away on their horses, and the princess waved them off.

Three days passed, and the men had not returned. On the fourth day the princess started to worry. On the fifth day she called all the women of the castle and said, 'Saddle your horses. We'll search for the prince and the men.'

The women galloped out of the castle to search the Dark Wood.

Next day, the prince and all the men arrived back at the castle. 'Where are the women?' they asked each other. 'There's no one here!' (The princess hadn't left a note, because no one could read or write in those days.)

'If they're not back by tomorrow morning, we'd better go and search for them!' declared the prince.

But next morning, they hadn't returned. So the men had breakfast (they didn't like getting their own, but they didn't have a choice), then galloped back to the Dark Wood again.

Two days later, the princess and the women came back. They were very tired, and very worried because they hadn't found the men.

'We'll rest for a day,' said the princess. (The prince hadn't left a note, either, for the reason explained before.) 'Then, if there's no sign of the men, we'll begin another search.'

The men didn't come back. So after a day's rest the princess and the women set off for the Dark Wood once more.

Two days after that . . . but there's no need to go on. So if ever you're walking in the Dark Wood, and you see a lot of *very* old men—or *very* old women—on *very* old horses, and they seem to be looking for someone . . .

Tell them, will you? Please?

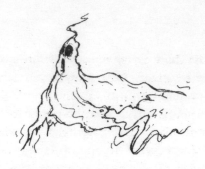

The Cabin Boy

The pirate captain was a wicked and ruthless man. He and his crew attacked countless ships, plundering their treasure, and they made everyone on board walk the plank until they fell off the end and the sharks—which were always waiting—said 'Yum!'

One day, they captured a ship with a young lad aboard. 'We need a new cabin boy,' said the captain. 'He'll do. Put him to work!'

The new cabin boy had to work like a dog, day and night. He was only small, and soon it was obvious that he wasn't up to it. When the captain found him asleep from sheer exhaustion, he was furious. 'He's useless!' he roared. 'I'll have no shirkers on my ship! Fetch the plank, me hearties—the sharks can have him!'

The boy wept and pleaded, but to no avail. He was prodded out on to the plank at sword point, and down below in the sea the sharks waited and said, 'Yum!'

As he fell off the plank and splashed into the sea, the heartless captain laughed. 'We'll find plenty more where he came from!'

They sailed on, looking for more ships to plunder.

Then on the third evening the wind dropped and the pirates were becalmed. As it grew dark, thick fog came rolling in, shrouding them in eerie grey. The sea was flat, and the only sounds were the creak of masts and rigging and the dull, damp flapping of the sails.

Suddenly the captain heard a splashing noise below him, as if the water was churning and bubbling. He looked over the rail . . . and screamed in terror.

For, climbing up the ship's side towards him was the ghost of the cabin boy. His eyes glared with a cold and terrible light. And behind him, dripping with water and draped with seaweed, came all the ghosts of all the captain's other victims.

The cabin boy laughed a horrible laugh, and his voice rang out in the fog:

'Fetch the plank, me hearties!' he cried to the ghostly sailors.

And down below in the water, the waiting sharks said, 'Yum!'

Silly Billy

Little Billy Bone
        Picked up a stone,
            And a voice said: '*I wouldn't do that . . .*'
He looked all about
For something to clout,
And the voice said: '*I wouldn't do that . . .*'
Billy took aim
At the window pane,
And the voice said: '*I wouldn't do that . . .*'
He got ready to throw,
And the voice said, '*Oh . . .*
I REALLY wouldn't do that . . .'
The stone went SMACK,
But the glass didn't crack,
The stone bounced back and hit Billy.
He dropped down dead,
And the little voice said:
'*I TOLD you that was silly!*'

The Girl in the Picture

The picture hanging in reception at the little country hotel showed the head of a girl with long plaits.

'It's very old,' said the hotel receptionist. 'We've no idea who she was. But look closely at her plaits. See? They're real hair.'

Alice was fascinated—and jealous. She had always wanted long plaits, but Mum wouldn't let her grow her hair. She kept staring at the picture. The girl didn't look very nice. She was glaring angrily, almost threateningly. But the plaits . . . Alice wanted plaits just like them. In fact, she decided when she lay in the hotel bed that night, she wanted *those* plaits. They were the same colour as her own hair. They'd look great on her.

So at midnight, she sneaked down to reception. The girl in the picture glared more furiously than ever, but Alice didn't care. She cut off the plaits and tied them to her own hair with bits of ribbon. She'd hide them in the morning, and no one would know what she'd done.

She was just falling asleep again when someone whispered in her ear.

'*Give them back.*'

Alice sat bolt upright in the dark. 'Who's there?'

'*Me*,' said the voice. '*You stole my plaits. Give them back.*'

I'm dreaming, thought Alice. There's no one here. There can't be. 'You don't scare me,' she said out loud.

'*Don't I?*' whispered the voice. And something tugged, hard, at one of Alice's new plaits.

'Ow!' cried Alice. 'Go away—you're not real.'

'Oh, yes I am,' said the voice. '*Want me to prove it?*' And each pull became more powerful and more painful as the voice snarled, '*Give—me—my—PLAITS!*'

They found Alice's body in the morning. But they never found her head. The hotel shut down, and no one ever goes in there now. The picture is still there, though. A girl's face, with real hair plaits. But she doesn't look angry any more. She looks scared.

And she looks a lot like Alice.

Well, Well

Flora lived in a little cottage, with her parents and seven brothers and sisters. There was a well at the bottom of their garden. One afternoon, Mother sent Flora to fetch water. Flora wound the bucket on its rope down into the well. She heard it splash in the water. Then:

'OUCH!' came an echoing voice from below. 'WHO DID THAT?'

Flora jumped, startled, then stared down into the well. But it was much too dark down there to see anything.

'Who's that?' she demanded.

'ME,' growled the voice. 'AND THIS IS MY WELL. GO AWAY!'

'It isn't your well!' said Flora indignantly. 'It's ours! And I want a bucket of water!'

'YOU CAN'T HAVE ONE,' said the voice. 'I'M HERE NOW, SO IT'S MY WELL. GO AWAY, OR YOU'LL BE SORRY!'

Flora was a very sensible girl, and she realized that someone was playing a trick on her. One of her brothers must have climbed down the well, she thought, and was trying to scare her. She'd show him what was what!

'You don't fool me,' she said. 'I know who you are. And when I've got my bucket of water, I'm going to put the wooden lid on the well, and you can stay there till tea-time!'

'YOU'D BETTER NOT,' the voice warned. 'YOU'LL BE *VERY* SORRY!'

'Ha!' snorted Flora. She grasped the rope and made ready to wind the full bucket up again.

From below, something *pulled*. And Flora tipped head first into the well.

The family heard her scream and came rushing out. They couldn't see Flora; she was in the well. All they saw were two huge, hairy hands grasping the rope, as *something* hauled itself up towards the daylight.

Mother shrieked, and Father rushed to the well and slammed the lid down hard. There was a furious yell, then a splash, then silence.

The family moved away that very day. And no one ever mentioned Flora's name again.

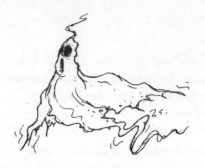

The Ghost at Ivy Cottage

I t was nearly dusk, and Mrs Smith was walking past the village playing field, when three girls came running out.

'Mrs Smith, Mrs Smith!' Nicky, Bryony, and Laura were breathless. 'Ivy Cottage is haunted!'

Ivy Cottage stood on its own on the other side of the field, behind a thick bramble hedge. Mrs Smith looked at the girls in surprise.

'Haunted? Whatever makes you think that?'

'We saw a light in there!' cried Nicky. 'Through the hedge! But nobody lives there, do they?'

'Well, it's for sale, and the people who own it have moved out,' said Mrs Smith. 'Perhaps the estate agent's showing someone round?'

'No, no!' insisted Bryony. 'It wasn't an ordinary light. It was *green* and it flickered.'

'And we heard something scream!' Laura added.

'Now, calm down!' Mrs Smith soothed. 'You're over-excited and scaring yourselves, that's all. There's no such thing as ghosts!'

'Sara says there is,' said Bryony. 'She told us Ivy Cottage is haunted.'

'Sara? Who's Sara?'

'Our friend. She's new.' The girls pointed to the playground gate. There was another girl standing there. Mrs Smith had never seen her before.

'Well, I think I'd better have a word with Sara.' Mrs Smith went over to the strange girl, and told her that she shouldn't go round scaring her new friends with silly stories.

'But it isn't silly,' said Sara. 'There *is* a ghost.'

'Right,' said Mrs Smith. 'Come with me, and I'll show you you're wrong and there's nothing to be frightened of.'

They all crossed the field. Ivy Cottage was just visible through the dense bramble hedge. There *was* a faint glow in one window, but it wasn't flickering.

'There,' said Mrs Smith. 'It's just an electric light. The owners must be back.'

Then suddenly the light turned a cold, strange green, and winked out. At the same moment, a weird cry echoed out of the dusk. Nicky, Bryony, and Laura screamed and ran away. Only Sara didn't run. She just stood staring at Mrs Smith.

'See?' she said.

Mrs Smith was shaken, but collected herself. 'Now, stop it,' she said. 'The light bulb went, that's all. And that noise must have been a bird; an owl, probably. There isn't a ghost!'

Sara said, 'Oh, yes, there is.'

She smiled at Mrs Smith. Then, very slowly, she faded away, until there was no one there.

Best Friends

I *like* you. I think you're really nice. And I want to be your friend.

You haven't got many friends; I've noticed that. You're a bit of a loner, really. Never mind. *I'm* here now. And I'll be the very best friend you've ever had.

People don't often see me. I'm very small, after all; and it's amazing how easy it is not to see something little, even when it's following right behind you. I follow you a lot, but you haven't noticed me yet. I wonder what you'll think, when you do? You might be frightened. A lot of people are. They run away, and later they tell themselves that they must have imagined what they saw. I'm ugly, you see. Very ugly, with my little hooked nose and my little warty face and my little clawed hands. And anyway, most people don't believe in us any more. They don't believe that the Little Folk exist.

But though I'm small, and I look ugly and frightening, I can be quite nice. I'm always nice to my friends. Though I don't like people who upset me. But you won't upset me. You're my friend, and I'm yours. So that's all right, isn't it? And if anyone upsets you . . . well, I won't be nice to them. I won't be nice *at all*. And I'm *very* good at being nasty, if I want to.

I *do* like you. I think I'll let you see me, soon. Don't be too frightened when I do. There's no need. Really there isn't. Because we're going to be friends for a very long time.

The best friends *ever*.

Scary Story

I'm writing a scary story.

Mum and Dad are out, and I'm upstairs in my room, writing my story on my computer. It's for school. All my class are writing stories, and tomorrow we'll read them out loud. My teacher, Mr Burns, says my stories are *really* scary. 'Joe,' he said last week, 'you ought to be a writer when you grow up. You even scare *me*.' I was really chuffed!

Anyway, in my story, this boy is alone in a creepy old house. It's dark, and something's after him. He can't see it, but he knows it's there. *Cre-e-eak* . . . There's a footstep on the stairs! His heart thumps. *Cre-e-eak* . . . It's coming closer! It's coming to get him! How can he get away? (He's in the attic; I forgot to tell you that.)

There's only one chance. He's got to go out on the stairs, confront the thing that's coming for him, and defeat it! It's a horrible thing: it looks like . . . Well, I haven't written that bit, yet. But it's really *ghoulish*. Is he brave enough to face it? (Of course he is; people in stories always are.) Now, how's he going to do it . . . ?

Cre-e-eak . . .

'Who's there?' Heart bumping.

Cre-e-eak . . . And, very softly, a horrible laugh . . .

No, you don't understand! I'm not writing my story now! I'm sitting in my room, with my hair standing on end, because—

Cre-e-eak . . .

—because there's something out there, on the stairs. I can hear it; and it just . . . *laughed.*

Mum and Dad aren't here. And I'm upstairs, and there's only one way out. Down the stairs. But there's something on the stairs. I heard it, I *did.* It laughed, and it went—

Cre-e-eak . . .

(Who's there?)

Cre-e-eak . . .

'Who's there?'

Cre-e-eak . . .

'WHO'S THERE . . . ?'

Knock, Knock, Who's There?

Jane was baby-sitting at the Joneses' for the first time. The house was a bit isolated down a long, dark lane, but the Joneses had made supper for her, and Kylie, their two year old, was very well behaved. Jane reckoned this was going to be a *great* job.

It was windy that night. Jane could hear the wind moaning round the house as she watched TV. Something outside kept rattling. It made her feel a bit nervous, because it sounded like someone knocking on the front door.

Rap . . . rap . . . rap . . . It was setting Jane's teeth on edge. She turned the TV down, wondering if Kylie might be making the noise. But there was no sound from upstairs.

Rap . . . rap . . . rap . . . It was coming from the hall . . . Jane's heart began to beat very fast. Someone *was* knocking on the door. Someone was outside, in the night, in the dark . . .

It took all her courage to venture to the hall. The front door had a low letterbox, and she remembered seeing a knocker fixed to it.

Rap . . . rap . . .

Jane drew in a frightened breath. Who was there? She didn't dare call out and ask. And she certainly didn't dare open the door.

Then she had an idea. If she looked out of the dining room window, she should be able to see whoever was knocking to get in. She ran to the room and peeked out.

There was nobody there.

She went back to the hall, wondering if she'd imagined it. But then:

Rap . . . rap . . . rap . . .

And Jane's eyes widened in horror as *something* lifted the flap of the letter box.

She opened her mouth to scream—

And from outside came a loud and clear, 'Miaow!'

Jane laughed aloud with relief. Of course, the Joneses had a cat—she'd seen the basket in the kitchen! And the knocker was low enough for a cat to reach. It must have learned to rap when it wanted to come in.

Full of confidence now, she opened the door. On the step was a sleek, gold-eyed tabby. It strolled into the house and she shut the door again.

'You gave me a fright!' she told the tabby. 'I thought there was a prowler there, or a ghost! But it was just a harmless old cat!'

The cat looked up at her. There was a funny light in its eyes, and it seemed to be grinning.

'Harmless?' it said. 'That's what *you* think!'

Beware of the Bears

A family were going backpacking in a National Park.

'Watch out for the bears,' the park ranger advised them. 'Black bears are OK; they mostly eat fruit. But the grizzly bears are dangerous.' He gave them each a small water-pistol. 'We call these Bear Safety Kits. If a grizzly comes at you, squirt him with it.' He grinned. 'It's full of Essence of Violets. Grizzly bears *hate* violets. So one squirt will make them run away.'

'How will we know if there are grizzlies around?' Mum asked nervously.

'Look for droppings,' said the park ranger. 'If you find some bear droppings and they've got fruit in them, you're safe. But if there's no fruit, watch out. Have a nice day, now!'

The family set off. They walked all morning along the park trails, and soon they found themselves in a beautiful pine wood. Then, ahead of them, they saw a pile of something on the path.

'Bear droppings!' said Dad. 'We'd better examine them for fruit.'

Joe and Beth giggled at that idea, but Dad crouched

down to take a look. He prodded the droppings with a stick and said, 'Oh–oh. There's no fruit here.'

Mum immediately started to rummage for her Bear Safety Kit. Joe and Beth were still peering at the droppings.

'What are those funny bright-coloured bits in it, then?' Beth wanted to know.

'And what's that smell?' said Joe. 'Phor! It's *horrible!*'

'Don't be silly,' said Mum. 'It's not horrible; it's nice. Violets.'

'Violets . . . ?' said everyone else uneasily.

'And those coloured bits . . . ' said Dad. 'They look like plastic. They look like . . . '

'Chewed up water pistols . . . ' said Joe and Beth, in very small voices.

Behind them, the undergrowth rustled hugely. And something *growled* . . .

Fairy Lullaby

One summer day, long ago, a young man was walking on a hilltop when he heard beautiful music coming from a nearby tree. Enchanted, he went to see who was playing. But there was no one there.

'It must be fairy music,' the young man told himself. 'How wonderful! I shall sit down under the tree and listen.'

He made himself comfortable. The music played on, and after a while the youth fell asleep.

When he woke, the music had stopped. And, to his surprise, the tree under which he sat was no longer green, but had withered and died.

How strange! he thought. Whatever could have happened to it?

Puzzled, he walked back home, where his family would be waiting for him. But when he saw the house, it looked different somehow. Surely the door should be blue, not red? And where had all that ivy on the walls come from?

As he hurried up the path, the door opened and a complete stranger came out. He greeted the young man and asked what he wanted.

'I live here!' cried the youth. 'Who are you? Where are my family? I left them here only a few hours ago!'

'Tell me,' said the stranger in alarm, 'what is your name?'

The youth told him—and the stranger's face turned deathly pale. 'My grandfather used to tell me about you,' he said in a quavering voice. 'You went out one morning and you vanished, never to return!'

'Your g-grandfather . . . ?' stammered the young man.

'Yes,' said the stranger. 'You were his son . . . '

In shock and distress, the stranger covered his eyes with his hands.

When he looked again, there was nothing but a pile of dust where the young man had stood.

Sticky Ending (6)

L ittle boat.
Nice and snug.
Brewing storm.
Glug–glug–glug.

Sticky Ending (7)

B uilding site.
No hard hat.
Falling plank.
Pity, that.

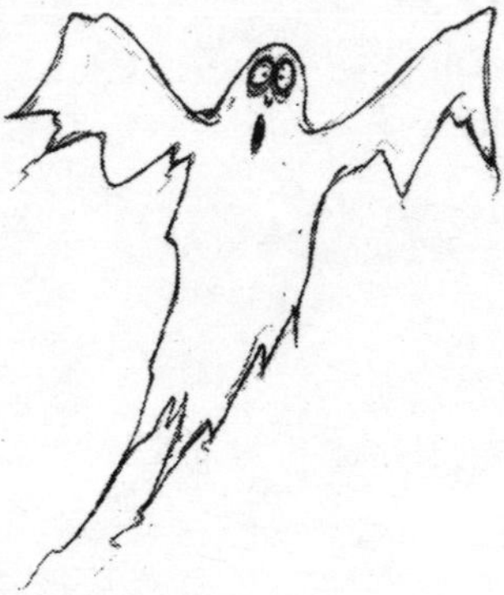